EARLY BIRD STORIES

Hoof on the Roof

Early ★ Reader

First American edition published in 2023 by Lerner Publishing Group, Inc.

An original concept by Cath Jones
Copyright © 2023 Cath Jones

Illustrated by Gisela Bohórquez

First published by Maverick Arts Publishing Limited

Maverick
arts publishing

Licensed Edition
Hoof on the Roof

Lerner Publications Company
An imprint of Lerner Publishing Group, Inc.
241 First Avenue North
Minneapolis, MN 55401 USA

For reading levels and more information, look up this title at www.lernerbooks.com.

Main body text set in Mikado a. Typeface provided by HVD Fonts.

Library of Congress Cataloging-in-Publication Data

Names: Jones, Cath, 1965– author. | Bohórquez, Gisela, illustrator.
Title: Hoof on the roof / Cath Jones ; illustrated by Gisela Bohórquez.
Description: First American edition. | Minneapolis : Lerner Publications, 2023. | Series: Early bird readers. Green (Early bird stories) | "First published by Maverick Arts Publishing Limited"— Page facing title page. | Audience: Ages 5–9. | Audience: Grades K–1. | Summary: "Lizzy is determined to reach the grass on the farmer's roof! This charming story's fun illustrations and text engage children as they learn to read"— Provided by publisher.
Identifiers: LCCN 2021055128 (print) | LCCN 2021055129 (ebook) | ISBN 9781728438474 (lib. bdg.) | ISBN 9781728448350 (pbk.) | ISBN 9781728444604 (eb pdf)
Subjects: LCSH: Readers (Primary) | LCGFT: Readers (Publications)
Classification: LCC PE1119.2 .J657 2023 (print) | LCC PE1119.2 (ebook) | DDC 428.6/2— dc23/eng/20211130

LC record available at https://lccn.loc.gov/2021055128
LC ebook record available at https://lccn.loc.gov/2021055129

Manufactured in the United States of America
2-1008874-49590-9/15/2022

Hoof on the Roof

Cath Jones

illustrated by
Gisela Bohórquez

Lerner Publications ◆ Minneapolis

Lizzy loved eating grass. She liked grass that was long, green, and fresh. But the grass in her field was short.

"I want to explore," said Lizzy.

The other cows helped Lizzy leave.

"Be careful," called the cows
as Lizzy trotted off down the road.

Soon Lizzy came to a farmhouse.

The roof was made of grass!

She mooed happily.

Lizzy spotted a ladder.

But Lizzy was big
and heavy.

SNAP!

The ladder broke in half!

"Sorry!" said Lizzy.

She looked up at the yummy grass roof.

Lizzy knocked on the farm door.

Hooves were good for knocking!

But nobody came out.

Lizzy sniffed.

The grass smelled so good!

She decided to borrow the digger.

But Lizzy's hooves made it tricky to brake.

Lizzy needed help to get onto the roof.

She set off to tell the other cows.

The cows were happy to see Lizzy.

"The farmer has a yummy grass roof," she said. "Come and see it!"

Lizzy and the cows ate the grass.

They danced with joy.

Clomp, clomp, clomp!

The farmer came out to see what the noise was.

When the farmer saw the cows,

he was amazed.

"Thank you for eating my grass," said the farmer. "You are better than a lawn mower!"

The farmer built a ramp for the cows
so they could always get to the grass.

Lizzy and the cows were happy on the roof. The farmer was happy too. He did not have to cut his grass!

Quiz

1. The grass in Lizzy's field was . . .
    a) Long
    b) Dirty
    c) Short

2. Why did Lizzy break the ladder?
    a) She was big and heavy
    b) She jumped on it
    c) She tripped on it

3. The grass on the roof smelled so . . .
    a) Bad
    b) Smelly
    c) Good

4. How did the cows get onto the roof?
   a) With a digger
   b) With a ladder
   c) By working together

5. What did the farmer build for the cows?
   a) A slide
   b) A ramp
   c) A barn

COLOR		GRL
Silver	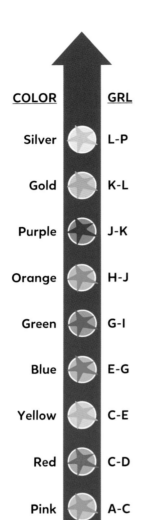	L-P
Gold		K-L
Purple		J-K
Orange		H-J
Green		G-I
Blue		E-G
Yellow		C-E
Red		C-D
Pink		A-C

Leveled for Guided Reading

Early Bird Stories have been edited and leveled by leading educational consultants to correspond with guided reading levels. The levels are assigned by taking into account the content, language style, layout, and phonics used in each book. Visit www.lernerbooks.com for more Early Bird Readers titles!